REDEEMER

(The Power and The Glory)

SONGBOOK 2

*Classical and Contemporary Songs
in Four Parts for
Orchestras, Choirs, Bands, Schools & Colleges*

Music and Lyrics

by

Dotun Adelekan

LECKSON
VENTURES

Published by
Leckson Ventures LLC
Sparks, Nevada. USA

E-mail : a_adelekan2000@hotmail.com
Web: www.dotunadelekan.com; www.redeemersongbook.com
Redeemer (The Power & The Glory) Songbook 2
© Dotun Adelekan. All rights reserved.

First Published in 2014
Cover design by Allen Jomoc
Interior Design by Dotun Adelekan

Library of Congress Cataloguing-in-Copyright Data

Dotun Adelekan – 1965
Redeemer, the Power and the Glory Songbook 2 – First Edition
Includes music, all additional lyrics, musical arrangement, and
entire sound recording.

Library of Congress Catalog Card Number : Pau 3-734-743

Effective Date of Registration : July 20, 2014

Published in the United States of America
ISBN : - 10 : 0-692-79417-4
ISBN : - 13 : 978-0-692-79417-3
1.Music/Educational
2.Music/Religious/Christian Gospel

DEDICATED

To All lovers of the Art of Musical Compositions as a way of expressing the beauty of our

Collective cultural heritage and appreciation of God's Glorious Creation!

Unto Him we return ALL The Praise for *His Habitation*

NO			PAGES

FOREWORD

By

Professor Aderemi Kuku Ph.D, FAMS(USA), FTWAS, FAAS, FAS (Nig) FMAN, OON, NNOM
President, African Academy of Sciences and Distinguished Professor of Mathematics and Computation Sciences, Botswana International University of Science and Technology(BIUST)

It is my great honour and priviledge to write this Foreword to the excellent Redeemer Song Book 2 by Dotun Adelekan. My family and I have been knowing Dotun , his parents and siblings for a very long time as members of the same Church—Oritamefa Baptist church, Ibadan , Nigeria. As such, we share the same faith in our Lord and Saviour, Jesus Christ, and hearing his musical compositions over the years has been a great source of spiritual upliftment and inspiration not only for me and my immediate family but also for all members of our Church. Indeed, Dotun has left an indelible mark in our Church as a prominent and influential member of our church Choir that has rendered many of his exciting compositions Sunday after Sunday, and during Easter and Christmas Cantatas. In fact, one of his most popular compositions "Lift him up" is song every Sunday by the whole congregation in our Church at Ibadan—it is printed in the Church bulletin every Sunday —and so he has left an everlasting legacy in our church family at Ibadan. Little wonder then that his life has been a spiritual inspiration for the younger generation to whom he has also been a great role model. His music is aired regularly by TV & Radio stations.

Dotun's many compositions have been based on actual scriptural verses from the old and new testaments, his own original wordings, and have taken various forms – Afro choral chorus, Hymns, recitations (soprano, baritones, etc), Alto aria, Tenor solo, Tenor and chorus, Quartet and chorus, Afrochorals-solo, Orchestra freedom opera, duet and chorus , classical music and so on. In short, his compositions have biblical and spiritual lessons for all and sundry and the Lord has used his songs for spiritual rebirth of many who come across him and his music

I am aware that the new Book has 80 new songs, a lot of which are focused on putting African musical heritage/culture on the orchestral stage in contemporary format. I recommend the contents of this book very highly for use in Concert performances,   Church services, Various Christian Fellowships , in Schools, Colleges and Universities, and also for radio and TV audiences and band performances.

It is my considered view that this book is a befitting tribute to Dotun's extraordinary musical talents that has been amply demonstrated in numerous ways even when he is not full time musician. That he is a practicing Engineer makes his musical achievements much more spectacular, and we thank God Almighty for giving him the grace to touch so many lives spiritually with his musical talents.

PREFACE

It's worth mentioning that some considerable time was used to sample people's opinion from all works of life on the pieces selections in Redeemer songbook one. The general consensus among young folks tend to favour having appetite for lots of 'toe tapping' contemporary pieces with also some moderate and matured interest in classical pieces as well in the older generation. The number of lovers of the classical styled music were significant , in fact some young listeners still feel classical pieces are nearer Heaven than the contemporary ones because of is solemnity, majestic nature and it's long standing association with the church over several years.

This being said, the author has repeatedly tried to create a balance and also a fusion between contemporary choral and classical choral categories. This fusion may be interpreted, if you like, as pieces having large scale orchestration with lively and majestic movements. Orchestrated pieces like 'Hosanna in the highest', 'Keresimesi de o' among others have an appreciation cutting across both musical styles with modern overtones. Arpeggiating the melodic line often creates lots of flexibility and ultimately have the tendency to naturally brighten up a dull melodic line using a blend of the two worlds with some 'head nods'.

 The challenge has been how best to express the musical 'head nodding' richness of the African culture in contemporary classical four part music setting, by using the correct interpretation of long existing different musical forms and presenting same on a modern day choral/band platform to stir an overwhelming appreciation during delightful rendition of the pieces. A musical form will naturally appeal best to the audience, the most at 'its roots'. Although diversity is also a key to unlocking complexities which in itself tend to have a wider audience with additional possibilities and opportunities because it's modelled to be 'all encompassing'.

In order to prevent unnecessary errors and re-set, great care has been taken not to reproduce any song, phrase or sequenced notes that has been produced by other composers and song writers, living or dead worldwide. The composer rarely listens to other composers works as much as he would have liked to. This in a sense prevents any conscious or uncounscious re-creation of existing ideas that may be interpreted as reproducing the works of others, but in fact endeavours to stay focus in actualising inspiration coming from the heart of hearts from the 'throne of grace'.

The works of other composers are greatly appreciated and respected, they having walked down the road several times before, while going on the journey. However nonetheless, any clash of musical sequence or phrase is highly regretted, it was not intentional. In fact, one morning i turned on the TV myself to get the days news highlights across the world as usual. While in the kitchen making myself some apple drink, a clash of phase attracted my attention on one of the international cable networks, when i heard one of the phrases within a sound track being played on TV. At first, i thought the composer of the piece played on TV copied mine phrase, whereas mine was not yet published at the time and at the same time i cannot recall hearing that piece before anywhere else. This is a good example of what i call a 'phrase lock' for a very short period.

The overall texture of some pieces, show the the six-four chords creating significant suspense leading to the dorminant chords or the augumented chords respectively, while using the beauty of the passing notes to create a 'catchy' leading voice. In some pieces, phrases and sequential movements can be very unpredictable as may be expected. No specific rule or best practice was followed. It was purely 'ad lib'.

Some modern day contemporary classics included has some repetivitive phrases but mostly with added variations and different movements and balanced periods. Most sweet/beautiful phrases tend to be repetitive in nature. Audience appreciation favours most times having a 'mind-sticky' phrase repeated after a rendition in their mind, rather than trying to remember more cumbersome , difficult to learn pieces in the first place and using unfit for purpose additional movements. Modern day pentecostal choruses tend to be of this repetitive nature as well. Many recorded songs religious or secular that have won various awards too fall into this category. Although no hard and fast rule was used in this work, whether to repeat a phrase or not, the composer is conscious of the fact that ' as beauty is in the eye of the beholder, so also good music is, in the ear of the listener and as such needed to make the best judgement possible at every point in time.

The best of the very best compositions, where ever made always end up on either the tv , the radio, the concert platform (indoor or open air gatherings) or mostly behind the pulpit to mention a few. The number of times phrases were repeated was very low in order to prevent monotony and boredom which could prevent effective communication. The simple truth is technically, the phrases were kept as simple as possible and the overall music sequence as melodic and as colourful as possible. The use of non repetitive phrases or period is seen in Redeemer Songbook three to mention some examples of variations to this fact.

Effective modulation was adopted enhamonically rather than modally most times, with a smooth return to the original tonic sometimes or a 'stay away' approach in the new key usually with one or more pivot chords as enablers. Chordal unity and variety were mostly introduced in the harmony to bring in the desired flavor of modern compositions. Tonal and thematic materials were deployed sometimes with added non-harmonic progressions to form a blend as necessary.

The rythmic texture of the Afrochoral pieces reflects the richness of the African ethnic music traditions with emphasis on the percussion instruments, which sometime has some very unique capability of changing patterns in an unpredictable manner but very smoothly quantized and almost an unnoticable change.

The Major scale, minor scale, melodic and harmonic scales were extensively used in different pieces as desired. Also the chromatic scale was used on few occasions on the lead voice to drive home the sequence more readily and introduce further varieties in the compositional style.

Another point to note on the Afrochoral is that there are over 2000 languages spoken in Africa for example. In some languages, the challenges come when the rise and fall of the note's different pitches dictates to a large extent the correct pronounciation of the word. In other words for the same word having two syllables, the meaning of the word could be different or wrongly represented just because the melodic line or musical progression moves from tonic to mediant and not the reverse direction that is, mediant to tonic, especially if the latter happens to be what is to be the lyric-message to be conveyed.

In order not to lose the message conveyed by the music however, it is important to blend the rise and fall of these notes with the correctly pronounced, carefully chosen spoken word. This introduced an additional factor considered during Afrochoral compositions and rendition in these languages in their different dialets. This precaution appears not to exist in the English Language or its more obvious when it occurs and have little effect on the meaning and accent.

In conclusion, the objective of this work is to introduce new dimensions of compositions into the Redeemer songbook series in order to create some varieties that will complement those already seen in songbook one of this series. Music composition is like a journey that leads to many destinations. You can choose to go in only one direction at a time and try out the others some other day!.

The author gracefully believes that words only, cannot express the great and mighty things that the Almighty God has accomplished for mankind at Calvary during His physical presence, dwelling and moving freely among us about two thousand years ago. And futher to this, the best piece of praise and worship possible, should be written for Him in recognition of the fundermentals of this great gesture for the redemption of mankind.

Unfortunately that glorious best of the very best piece is still yet to come. Aspiring to get to it someday by His special grace and anointing!.

Dotun Adelekan

Cairo, Egypt 2014

ACKNOWLEDGEMENTS

I acknowledge the support and encouragement of friends and well-wishers and senior friends who make time out of their busy schedule to attend the concerts rendition of these works in honor of the LORD's Name from time to time.

May God continue to bless you the more as you continuously make time to glorify His Most Holy Name. Amen.

Above all, praise and thanks to God for inspiration, vision and strength to sustain this series of works.

Also to the LORD Jesus Christ the King of Kings and the LORD of Lords! In Him dwells the fullness of the God Head bodily.

PART I

1. INSTRUMENTALS - OVERTURE

FLOWING ♩ = 80

DOTUN ADELEKAN

2. HIGH PRAISE - HOSSANA IN THE HIGHEST

DOTUN ADELEKAN

3. AFROCHORALE10 - ARA E WOLE FUN

DOTUN ADELEKAN

4. INTROIT AFROCHORAL - ARA E WA

DOTUN ADELEKAN

5. SONG & CHORUS - A CROWN OF LIFE

DOTUN ADELEKAN

5. SONG & CHORUS - A CROWN OF LIFE

STRU - GGLE ___ THERE RE - MAIN A CROWN OF LIFE ___ FOR THOSE WHO BE - LIEVE

IT WON'T BE LONG ___ OUR DREAMS COME TRUE ___ OUR FAITH RE - NEWED ___

5. SONG & CHORUS - A CROWN OF LIFE

5. SONG & CHORUS - A CROWN OF LIFE

5. SONG & CHORUS - A CROWN OF LIFE

6. AFROCHORAL40 - BABA O WA!

DOTUN ADELEKAN

7. CHORUS - BABA OPE YE O

DOTUN ADELEKAN

Repeat and Fade

8. CHORUS - BETHLEHEM EPHRATAH

DOTUN ADELEKAN

DOTUN ADELEKAN

8. CHORUS - BETHLEHEM EPHRATAH

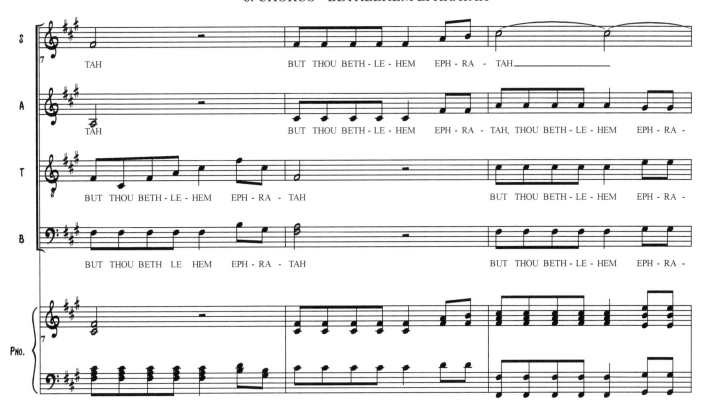

8. CHORUS - BETHLEHEM EPHRATAH

8. CHORUS - BETHLEHEM EPHRATAH

8. CHORUS - BETHLEHEM EPHRATAH

8. CHORUS - BETHLEHEM EPHRATAH

8. CHORUS - BETHLEHEM EPHRATAH

8. CHORUS - BETHLEHEM EPHRATAH

8. CHORUS - BETHLEHEM EPHRATAH

S: LI - TTLE A - MONG THE THOU - SAND OF JU DAH

A: LI - TTLE A - MONG THE THOU_____ SAND OF JU - DAH

T: LI - TTLE A - MONG THE THOU_____ SAND OF JU - DAH

B: LI - TTLE A - MONG THE____ THOU - SAND OF JU - DAH

9. CHORUS - READ YOUR BIBLE PRAY

10. SONG - BLESSED IS THE KING

DOTUN ADELEKAN

IN THE NAME OF THE LORD

11. CHORUS - WE WANT THE WHOLE WORLD

DOTUN ADELEKAN

12. SONG - PRAISE HIM ALL YE PEOPLE

- DOTUN ADELEKAN -

13. TENOR SONG - NEVER ALONE

DOTUN ADELEKAN

14. TENOR SOLO - WHERE WERE YOU ?

WITH CONVICTION ♩ = 95

DOTUN ADELEKAN

15. AFROCHORAL - E JE KA F'OKAN

MODERATO ♩ = 60

DOTUN ADELEKAN

1.E JE KA F'O - KAN FUN BA-BA O

E JE KA FI - YIN F'O - LU - WA O   E JE KA WO - LE FUN BA-BA O

© - DOTUN ADELEKAN -

16. CHORUS - KERESIMESI DE O

DOTUN ADELEKAN

16. CHORUS - KERESIMESI DE O

16. CHORUS - KERESIMESI DE O

16. CHORUS - KERESIMESI DE O

16. CHORUS - KERESIMESI DE O

16. CHORUS - KERESIMESI DE O

16. CHORUS - KERESIMESI DE O

16. CHORUS - KERESIMESI DE O

Double Chorus Feel Orchestration

17. SONG - CELEBRATION OF PRAISE

DOTUN ADELEKAN

Lyrics in score:

SA - VIOUR A - DO - NAI YOU CAME IN - TO MY LIFE TO SET ME
GLO - RY AND HO - NOUR BLESS THE LORD MY SOUL AND GIVE HIM

18. AFROCHORAL43 - AJINDE ENI MIMO

DOTUN ADELEKAN

19. CHORUS - WE WILL REMEMBER

19. CHORUS - WE WILL REMEMBER

20. CHORUS - CORONATION 2

PSALM 112/148

DOTUN ADELEKAN

20. CHORUS - CORONATION 2

CREA-TURES HERE BE-LOW PRAISE HIM ALL YE STARS IN HEAV'N PRAISE HIM FOR HIS FAITH-FUL-NESS

CREA-TURES HERE BE-LOW PRAISE HIM ALL YE STARS IN HEAV'N PRAISE HIM FOR HIS FAITH-FUL-NESS

CREA-TURES HERE BE-LOW___ PRAISE HIM ALL YE STARS IN HEAV'N PRAISE HIM FOR HIS FAITH-FUL-NESS

CREA-TURES HERE BE-LOW___ PRAISE HIM ALL YE STARS IN___ HEA-VEN PRAISE HIM FOR HIS FAITH-FUL-NESS

THY WILL BE DONE ON EARTH AND IN HEAV'N BE-FORE THE THRONE LET THE GLO-RY OF THE LORD DE-SCEND PRAISE YE THE

THY WILL BE DONE ON EARTH AND IN HEAV'N BE-FORE THE THRONE LET THE GLO-RY OF THE LORD DE-SCEND PRAISE YE THE

THY WILL BE DONE ON EARTH AND IN HEAV'N BE-FORE THE THRONE LET THE GLO-RY OF THE LORD DE-SCEND PRAISE YE THE

THY WILL BE DONE ON EARTH AND IN HEAV'N BE-FORE THE THRONE LET THE GLO-RY OF THE LORD DE-SCEND PRAISE YE THE

20. CHORUS - CORONATION 2

20. CHORUS - CORONATION 2

20. CHORUS - CORONATION 2

20. CHORUS - CORONATION 2

20. CHORUS - CORONATION 2

PART II

21. MEDLEY - WALL OF JERICHO

Joshua 6 **HIGHLY SPIRITED** ♩ = 110

DOTUN ADELEKAN

Synth Brass 1 *Now Jericho was shut up because of the children of Isreal, none went out, & non went in. & the LORD said unto Joshua*

see, i have given into thine hand Jericho, & the king thereof, & the mighty men of valour. & ye shall compass the city, all ye men of

war & go round about the city once, thus shall thou do 6 days. And seven priest shall bear before the ark 7 trumpets of ram horns

and the seventh day ye shall compass the city 7 times, and the priests shall blow the trumpets. And it shall come to pass when they make a long blast with the ram's horn; and when ye hear the sound of the trumpet, all the people shall shout with a great shout; &

the wall of the city shall fall down flat!. And it came to pass when Joshua has spoken to the people that the seven priests bearing the seven trumpets of rams horn passed on before the LORD, & blew the trumpets: and the ark of the convenant of the LORD followed

& Joshua had commanded the people saying ye shall not shout, nor make noise with your voice, neither shall ye speak a word out

until the 7th day as i told you. So the ark of the LORD compassed the city, going about it once:& they came into the camp & lodged.

And Joshua rose early in the morning, & the priests took up the ark of the LORD & 7 priests bearing seven trumpets of rams'horn

before the ark of the LORD went continually, & blew the trumpets: & the armed men went before them with the re-reward aft the ark

And the second day they compassed the city once, & returned into the camp: so they did six days. And it came to pass on the 7th day

they went round the city 7 times. And at the seventh time, when the priests blew the trumpets, Joshua said unto the people with joy

shout, shout, shout for the LORD has given you the city! Boys

HA-LLE-LU - JAH HA-LLE-LU - JAH HA-LLE-

HA-LLE-LU - JAH HA-LLE-LU - JAH HA-LLE-

A Tempo - Marching Style

Girls

with a great shout, and the wall, the wall fell down flat!!!

22. SONG - EARLY IN THE MORNING

DOTUN ADELEKAN

23. SONG - FILL ME LORD

MODERATELY ♩ = 75

DOTUN ADELEKAN

24. SONG - MAKE US THINE LORD

DOTUN ADELEKAN

Psalm 90 : 12-13

25. AFROCHORAL3 - E GBE JESU GA !

DOTUN ADELEKAN

TRADITIONAL TYLE ♩ = 85

26. CHORUS - FOR GOD SO LOVED THE WORLD

DOTUN ADELEKAN

27. CHORUS - FOR THE LORD HIMSELF

1 THESSALONIANS CHAPT. 4 :16 &17

DOTUN ADELEKAN

27. CHORUS - FOR THE LORD HIMSELF

27. CHORUS - FOR THE LORD HIMSELF

27. CHORUS - FOR THE LORD HIMSELF

27. CHORUS - FOR THE LORD HIMSELF

28. AFROCHORAL13 - BABA L'O GBE O GA

DOTUN ADELEKAN

28. AFROCHORAL13 - BABA L'O GBE O GA

28. AFROCHORAL13 - BABA L'O GBE O GA

28. AFROCHORAL13 - BABA L'O GBE O GA

28. AFROCHORAL13 - BABA L'O GBE O GA

28. AFROCHORAL13 - BABA L'O GBE O GA

28. AFROCHORAL13 - BABA L'O GBE O GA

28. AFROCHORAL13 - BABA L'O GBE O GA

28. AFROCHORAL13 - BABA L'O GBE O GA

28. AFROCHORAL13 - BABA L'O GBE O GA

28. AFROCHORAL13 - BABA L'O GBE O GA

HA-LLE, HA-LLE, HA-LLE, HA-LLE, E - MI - MI - MO, E - MI - MI - MO, E - MI - MI - MO GBO - HUN___ RE!

HA-LLE, HA-LLE, HA-LLE, HA-LLE, E - MI - MI - MO, E - MI - MI - MO, E - MI - MI - MO GBO - HUN___ RE!

HA-LLE, HA-LLE, HA-LLE, HA-LLE, JE - SU E - MI - MI - MO, E - MI - MI - MO, GBO - HUN RE!

HA-LLE, HA-LLE, HA-LLE, HA-LLE, E - MI - MI - MO E - MI - MI - MO, E - MI - MI - MO, GBO - HUN RE!

29. AFROCHORALE 4 - GBE GA L'OHUN RARA

DOTUN ADELEKAN   DOTUN ADELEKAN

29. AFROCHORALE 4 - GBE GA L'OHUN RARA

29. AFROCHORALE 4 - GBE GA L'OHUN RARA

29. AFROCHORALE 4 - GBE GA L'OHUN RARA

29. AFROCHORALE 4 - GBE GA L'OHUN RARA

29. AFROCHORALE 4 - GBE GA L'OHUN RARA

29. AFROCHORALE 4 - GBE GA L'OHUN RARA

30. SONG - COUNT YOUR MANY BLESSINGS

DOTUN ADELEKAN

31. TENOR SOLO - IT IS FINISHED

DOTUN ADELEKAN

32. CHORUS - MYSTERY BABEL

DOTUN ADELEKAN

OH WAH-WAH BA-BEL OH___ MY - STERY BA-BEL THE

GREAT MO-THER OF HAR-LOTS AND OF I - DOL WOR-SHIP E-VERY-

WHERE A-ROUND THE WORLD MY-STERY BA-BEL WOW WOW! MY-STREY BA-BEL WOW WOW!

MY-STERY BA - BEL WOW! WOW! MY-STERY BA - BEL MY-STERY BA - BEL WOW! WOW!

34. SONG - HOLY, HOLY, HOLY LORD GOD

CHORUS

35. AFROCHORALE 50 - PRAISE HIM, PRAISE HIM

DOTUN ADELEKAN

DOTUN ADELEKAN & PUBLIC DOMAIN

PRAISE HIM PRAISE HIM OH PRAISE HIM PRAISE HIM PRAISE HIM PRAISE HIM OH PRAISE HIM PRAISE HIM

PRAISE HIM PRAISE HIM OH PRAISE HIM PRAISE HIM PRAISE HIM PRAISE HIM OH PRAISE HIM PRAISE HIM

35. AFROCHORALE 50 - PRAISE HIM, PRAISE HIM

35. AFROCHORALE 50 - PRAISE HIM, PRAISE HIM

35. AFROCHORALE 50 - PRAISE HIM, PRAISE HIM

35. AFROCHORALE 50 - PRAISE HIM, PRAISE HIM

35. AFROCHORALE 50 - PRAISE HIM, PRAISE HIM

35. AFROCHORALE 50 - PRAISE HIM, PRAISE HIM

35. AFROCHORALE 50 - PRAISE HIM, PRAISE HIM

35. AFROCHORALE 50 - PRAISE HIM, PRAISE HIM

36. AFROCHORALE49 - IROHIN ANA !

TRADITIONAL STYLE ♩= 100

DOTUN ADELEKAN

37. SONG - JESUS IS THE SAME

WITH FEELINGS ♩=80

DOTUN ADELEKAN

38. CHORUS - WHO IS LIKE UNTO THEE?

DOTUN ADELEKAN

39. HYMN - VICTORY OVER THE GRAVE

DOTUN ADELEKAN

40. CHORUS - JUBILATE !

DOTUN ADELEKAN   Xmas   DOTUN ADELEKAN

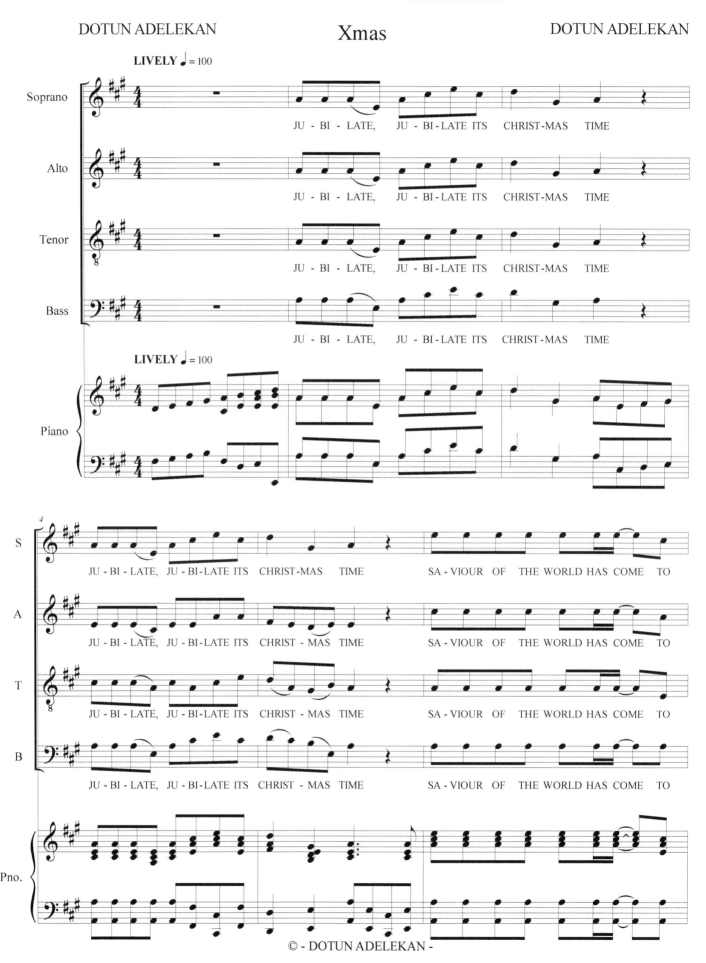

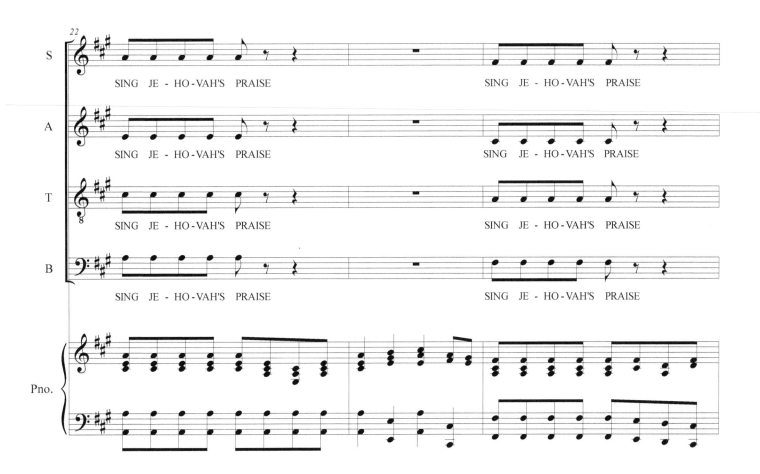

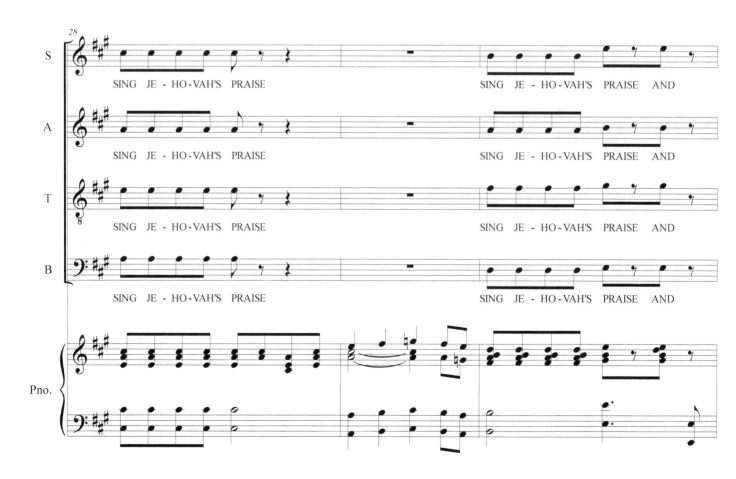

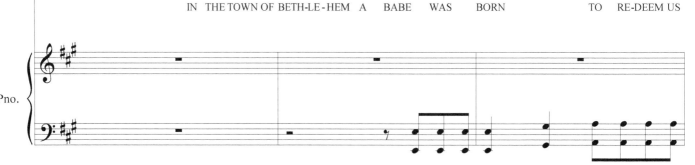

PART III

41. SONG - SING UNTO THE LORD

DOTUN ADELEKAN

42. CHORUS - KEEP ON SINGING

DOTUN ADELEKAN

CONTEMPORARY GOSPEL ♩ = 85

Soprano Alto: 1.E - VE - RY - THING IS GO - NA BE AL - RIGHT ___ E - VE - RY - THING IS GO - NNA BE AL - RIGHT

1.E - VE - RY - THING IS GO - NA BE AL - RIGHT ___ E - VE - RY - THING IS GO - NNA BE AL - RIGHT

HE IS THE KING OF GLO - RY HE IS THE RIGH - TEOUS ONE ___

43. SONG - LIFE AT ITS BEST

1.LIFE___ AT ITS BEST   IS A   LIFE___ WITH CON - TROL   LIFE THAT   IS LIVED   BY A

SPRING THAT SHALL NE'ER RUN DRY_____
LIFE_____ OF WAS - TED
YEARS_____

44. CHORUS - SET MY SPIRIT FREE

DOTUN ADELEKAN

NAME   E - MMA - NU - EL _____   EL _____
NAME   E - MMA - NU - EL _____

45. SOP&BASS DUET - O GOD OF ALL AGES !

DOTUN ADELEKAN

46. AFROCHORAL25 - OGO IYIN OLA

DOTUN ADELEKAN

BA-BA__ E MA SE_____ A__ DU-PE O-MO__ O-SE - UN O A__ DU-PE BA-BA

Repeat & Fade

1, 2, 3.

BA-BA__ E MA SE_____ A__ DU-PE O-MO__ O-SE - UN O

1, 2, 3.

1, 2, 3.

47. SONG - WE GIVE OUR PRAISE TO GOD

DOTUN ADELEKAN

48. SONG - I AM MOVING ON

DOTUN ADELEKAN

49. SONG - YOU LOOK AROUND THE WORLD

DOTUN ADELEKAN

50. CHORUS - REJOICE, REJOICE, REJOICE

DOTUN ADELEKAN

DOTUN ADELEKAN

WOMEN & TENOR   + BARITONE

50. CHORUS - REJOICE, REJOICE, REJOICE
THIRD RUN

50. CHORUS - REJOICE, REJOICE, REJOICE

51. SONG - RISE AND BE HEALED

DOTUN ADELEKAN

DOTUN ADELEKAN

52. TENOR - REJOICE O YE RIGHTEOUS

DOTUN ADELEKAN

53. SONG - LET ALL THE PEOPLE REJOICE

Psalm 111 : 1-4

DOTUN ADELEKAN

3

54. SONG - YOU ARE THE ONE

YOU ARE THE BONE OF MY BONE_____ YOU ARE THE FLESH OF MY FLESH_____ YOU'RE THE

ONE FOR ME_____ SINCE I SET MY EYES ON YOU_____ YOU ARE MY LOVE_____

Aaa_____

_____YOU ARE MY FRIEND AND MY ALL!_____ YOU ARE THE ONE THAT I WANT_____

Soprano Solo

Flute_____

YOU ARE THE FLESH OF MY FLESH____ YOU'RE THE ONE FOR ME__ SINCE I SET MY EYES ON YOU__

YOU ARE MY LOVE_____ YOU ARE MY FRIEND AND MY ALL!__

55. SONG - THANK YOU FOR THE MUSIC

DOTUN ADELEKAN

ITS GOOD TO PRAISE THE LORD ITS GOOD TO BLESS HIS NAME ITS GOOD TO CLAP YOUR HANDS____ ON THIS

DAY OF GLAD___ NESS ON THIS DAY OF___ PEACE   TO HIS__ NAME___ ALL OUR PRAISE BE - LONG

THANK YOU FOR THE MU - SIC   YOU HAVE GI-VEN TO US   THANK YOU FOR THE POW'R____ YOU HAVE

56. SONG - THANK YOU FOR CREATING ME

57. CHORUS - LET REVIVAL FLOW

DOTUN ADELEKAN

58. SONG - ALL GLORY AND PRAISE TO JESUS

DOTUN ADELEKAN

59. ANTHEM - THE BEAUTY OF ISREAL

2 SAMUEL CHAPT. 1 VRS 19-23

DOTUN ADELEKAN

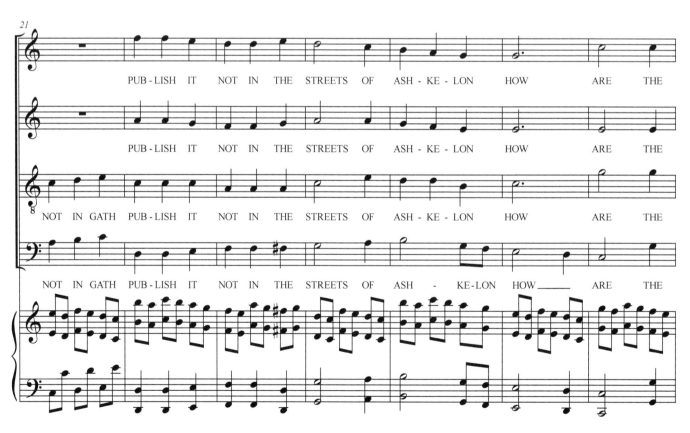

60. CHORUS - TOMMORROW

DOTUN ADELEKAN

MAY NE-VER COME O_____ MY FRIEND GIVE YOUR LIFE___ O_____ TO JE-SUS TO-DAY

PART IV

61. OVERTURE - KIDDIES !

DOTUN ADELEKAN

a tempo

62. SONG - THOU ART WORTHY TO TAKE THE BOOK

DOTUN ADELEKAN

63. CHORUS - THE LORD IS RISEN

DOTUN ADELEKAN

64. AFROCHORAL17 - REVIVE THY WORK

HABAKKUK:3:2

DOTUN ADELEKAN

65. HYMN - COME THOU LORD JESUS

66. SONG - FOR UNTO US A CHILD IS BORN

DOTUN ADELEKAN

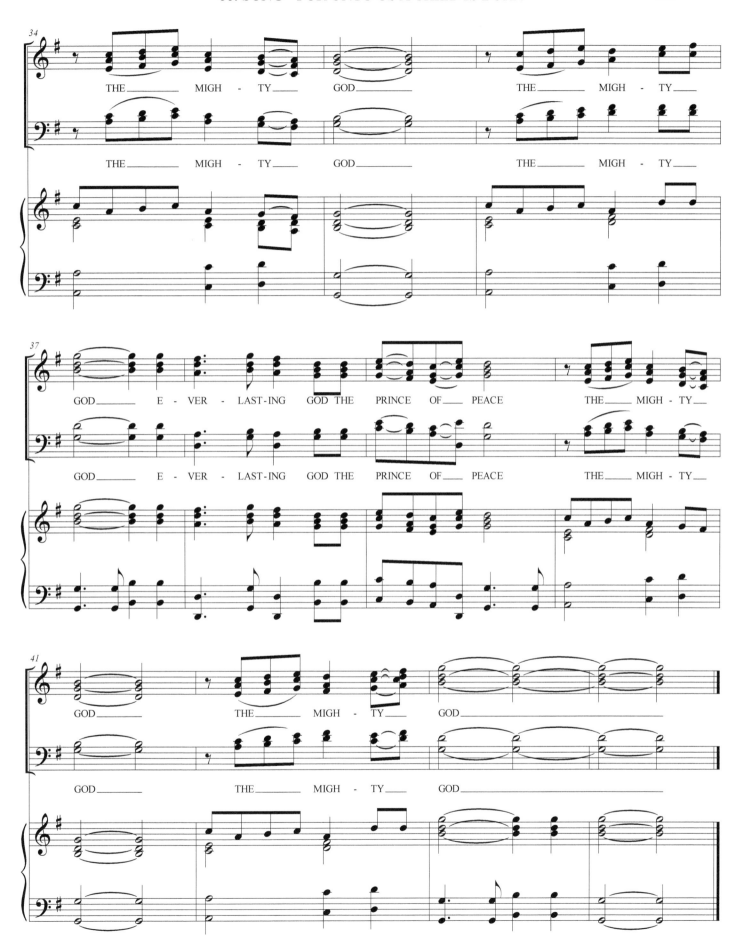

67. SONG - JESUS REIGNS, JESUS RULES

DOTUN ADELEKAN

68. AFROCHORAL14 - OBA ALADEE WU RA

DOTUN ADELEKAN

68. AFROCHORAL14 - OBA ALADEE WU RA

68. AFROCHORAL14 - OBA ALADEE WU RA

68. AFROCHORAL14 - OBA ALADEE WU RA

68. AFROCHORAL14 - OBA ALADEE WU RA

68. AFROCHORAL14 - OBA ALADEE WU RA

68. AFROCHORAL14 - OBA ALADEE WU RA

68. AFROCHORAL14 - OBA ALADEE WU RA

68. AFROCHORAL14 - OBA ALADEE WU RA

68. AFROCHORAL14 - OBA ALADEE WU RA

69. CHORUS - RISE UP ISREAL

DOTUN ADELEKAN

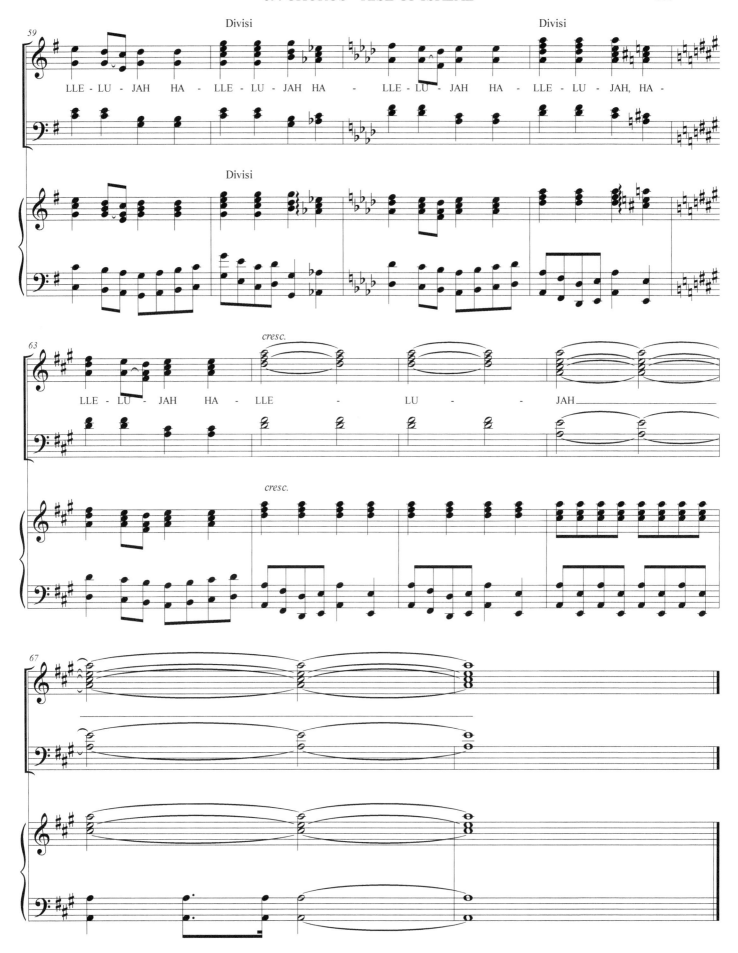

70. SONG - SOMEBODY TELL THEM

DOTUN ADELEKAN

71. AFROCHORAL16 - ELERU IYIN

DOTUN ADELEKAN

72. FAMILY LIFE - TIME OUT

DOTUN ADELEKAN

73. SONG - BEHOLD I STAND AT THE DOOR ⁴¹⁹

REVELATION CHAPT. 3 VRS 20

DOTUN ADELEKAN

ON HIS NA - ME YOU WILL TRUST IF THIS CHANCE WAS

NOT GI - VEN TO YOU WHAT CAN YOU DO?

IF THIS CHANCE WAS NOT GI - VEN TO YOU WHAT WILL YOU

74. SONG - HALLELUJAH TO THE LORD

WORSHIPFULLY ♩ = 90

DOTUN ADELEKAN

1.HA - LLE - LU - JAH, HA - LLE - LU - JAH, HA - LLE -
LU - JAH TO THE LORD THANK YOU JE - SUS FOR'ALL THE
THINGS YOU HAVE DONE _____ HE IS

75. CHORUS - GIVE IT UP TODAY !

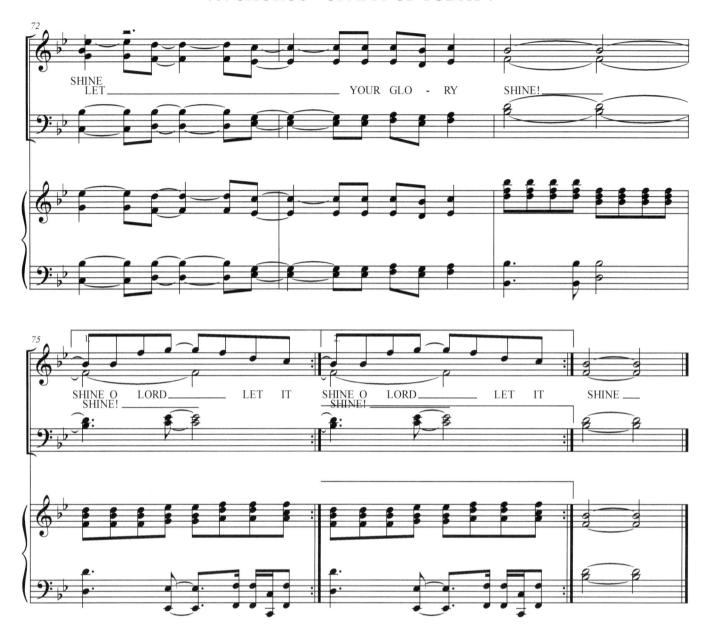

76. HYMN - GUIRD UP YOUR LOINS

DOTUN ADELEKAN

77. MUSICAL - W'ARE ON OUR WAY !

IN CONTEMPORARY MUSICAL STYLE ♩ = 120

DOTUN ADELEKAN

FORE WE ALL A-RRIVE   IS   NO-THING WHEN COM-PARED TO   ALL THAT   GOD HAS DONE FOR US

Bells

Narrator: The children of Isreal journed to the wilderness of Sinai

where they pitched tents and camped before the mountains   *Moses went up to God*

while the host of Isreal   remained and continued in their rebellious acts against Jehovah God!

Voice1: Hey boy, fancy beards has gone to the mountains lets make fun

V2: of him?. V1: Yes, get the other guys! v3: You wanna sin against God the more ? V2: Thats your headac

TO GLO - RY LAND

78. CHORUS - IT WON'T BE LONG

79. CHORUS - W'RE MATCHING ON

DOTUN ADELEKAN

80. CHORUS - GLORY TO HIS NAME

DOTUN ADELEKAN

80. CHORUS - GLORY TO HIS NAME

80. CHORUS - GLORY TO HIS NAME

Lightning Source UK Ltd.
Milton Keynes UK
UKHW051842081220
374827UK00011B/869